A BEASTY STORY

A BEASTY STORY

HUFF
PUFF
HUFF
PUFF
HUFF
PUFF
HUFF
PUFF
HUFF
PUFF

SNIPPETY
SNICK
SNIPPETY
SNICK
SNIPPETY
SNICK

NICK 5

HANK 6

Bill Martin Jr & Steven Kellogg

SCHOLASTIC INC.

New York Toronto London Auckland Sydney
Mexico City New Delhi Hong Kong

ISBN 0-439-21092-5

Original text copyright © 1970 by Harcourt Brace & Company/Copyright renewed 1998 by Bill Martin Jr. This edition: Text copyright 1999 by Bill Martin Jr. and Steven Kellogg. Illustrations copyright © 1999 by Steven Kellogg. All rights reserved. Published by Scholastic Inc., 555 Broadway, New York, NY 10012, by arrangement with Harcourt Brace & Company. SCHOLASTIC and associated logos are trademarks and/or registered trademarks of Scholastic Inc.

12 11 10 9 8 7 6 5 4 3 2 1   0 1 2 3 4 5/0

Printed in the U.S.A.   08

First Scholastic printing, September 2000

With love and appreciation
to Michael Sampson and his family
—B. M. & S. K.

It's getting DARKER.
And DARKER.
And DARKER!
Let's light our candles!

In a dark, dark wood
there is a dark, dark house.

In the dark brown house
there is a dark, dark stair.

there is a dark, dark cellar.

there is a dark, dark cupboard.

there is a dark, dark bottle.

There is something inside

the dark green bottle.

A BEAST!

It floats out of the dark green bottle,

through the dark purple cupboard,

across the dark blue cellar,

up the dark red stair,

out of the dark brown house,

through the dark, dark wood,

toward an even DARKER house,

where a *white* beast rises

and GRABS HIM!

There is a flash of light!

sounds of beasty laughter,

followed by beasty snores.

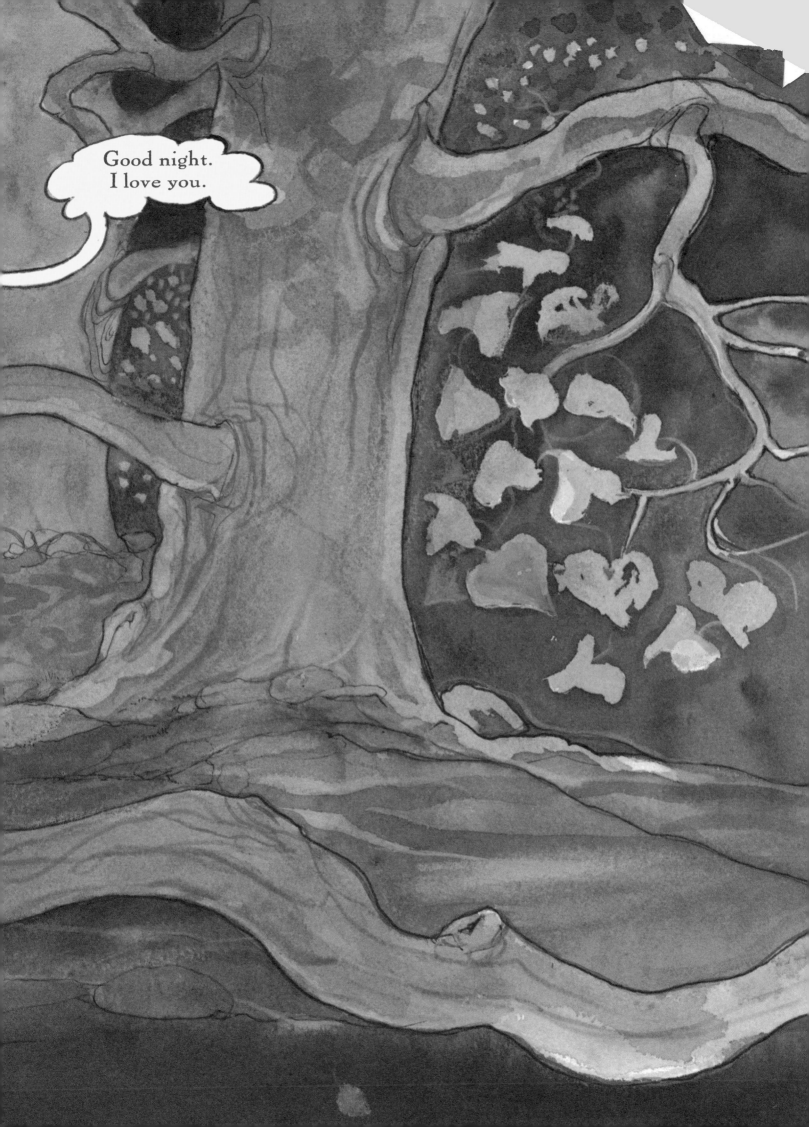